In the Half Room

Carson Ellis

Half chair

Half hat

Two shoes,

each half

Half table

Half cat

Half a window

Half a door

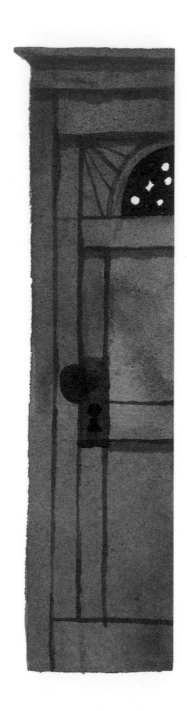

Half a rug on half a floor

The light of the half moon

shines down on the half room.

Half flowers
in half a vase

Half a book

Half a face

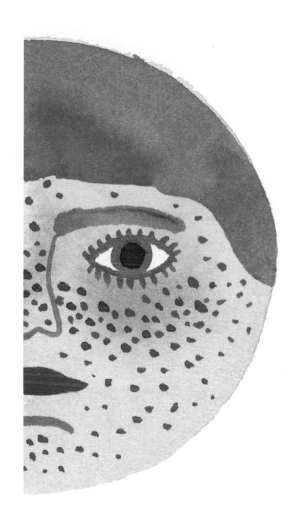

Half a moon

in a half-moon phase

Half a rug on half a floor

Half a face

you've seen before.

SHOOOOOP

Half lamp
Half light

Two half shoes
in the half
moonlight

Half a rug on half a floor

Half a cat is at the door.

Two half cats
in a half-cat fight

Two half cats asleep

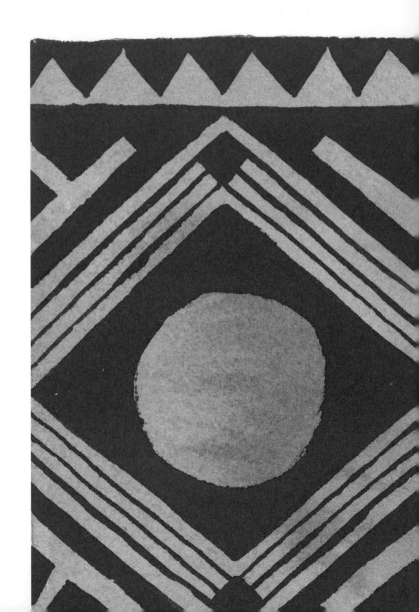

Good night!

The End

This book is for my son Milo. He gave me the idea for it and cheered me on while I made it, even though he's not sure about the ending. This book is also for my cats, past and present: Couscous, Kip, Alice, China, Albert, Fortinbras, Window, and Moony. Muses, all.

 First edition 2020. Library of Congress Catalog Card Number pending. ISBN 978-1-5362-1456-7. This book was typeset in Normande Standard Italic. The illustrations were done in gouache. Candlewick Press, 99 Dover Street, Somerville, Massachusetts 02144. www.candlewick.com. Printed in Shenzhen, Guangdong, China. 20 21 22 23 24 25 CCP 10 9 8 7 6 5 4 3 2 1